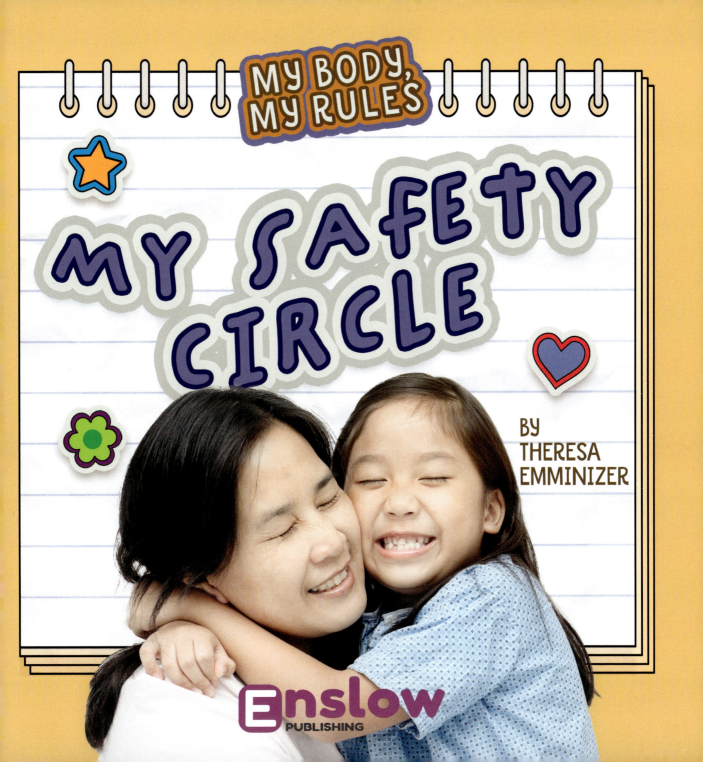

Please visit our website, www.enslow.com.
For a free color catalog of all our high-quality books, call toll free
1-800-398-2504 or fax 1-877-980-4454.

Library of Congress Cataloging-in-Publication Data

Names: Emminizer, Theresa, author.
Title: My safety circle / Theresa Emminizer.
Description: [Buffalo] : Enslow Publishing, [2025] | Series: My body, my
   rules | Includes bibliographical references and index. | Audience:
   Grades K-1
Identifiers: LCCN 2023053922 (print) | LCCN 2023053923 (ebook) | ISBN
   9781978539501 (library binding) | ISBN 9781978539495 (paperback) | ISBN
   9781978539518 (ebook)
Subjects: LCSH: Children and adults–Juvenile literature. | Trust–Juvenile
   literature. | Children and strangers–Juvenile literature.
Classification: LCC BF723.A33 E46 2025 (print) | LCC BF723.A33 (ebook) |
   DDC 613.6–dc23/eng/20231201
LC record available at https://lccn.loc.gov/2023053922
LC ebook record available at https://lccn.loc.gov/2023053923

Published in 2025 by
Enslow Publishing
2544 Clinton Street
Buffalo, NY 14224

Copyright © 2025 Enslow Publishing

Designer: Tanya Dellaccio Keeney
Editor: Theresa Emminizer

Photo credits: Series art (notebook) Design PRESENT/Shutterstock.com; series art (stickers) tmn art/Shutterstock.com; cover (people) kwanchai.c/Shutterstock.com; p. 5 Hananeko_Studio/Shutterstock.com; p. 7 Sharomka/Shutterstock.com; p. 9 fizkes/Shutterstock.com; p. 11 Evgeny Atamanenko/Shutterstock.com; p. 13 Gecko Studio/Shutterstock.com; p. 15 Pond Saksit/Shutterstock.com; p. 17 PeopleImages.com - Yuri A/Shutterstock.com; p. 19 Prostock-studio/Shutterstock.com; p. 21 wavebreakmedia/Shutterstock.com.

All rights reserved.
No part of this book may be reproduced in any form without permission in writing from the publisher, except by a reviewer.

Printed in the United States of America

Some of the images in this book illustrate individuals who are models. The depictions do not imply actual situations or events.

CPSIA compliance information: Batch #CSENS25: For further information contact Enslow Publishing, at 1-800-398-2504.

CONTENTS

WHAT'S A SAFETY CIRCLE? 4
WHO'S IN IT? 6
SARAH STAYS SAFE 8
THE THREE U'S. 10
WILLA'S WARNING SIGNS 12
FEELINGS ARE FRIENDS. 14
SHARE YOUR FEELINGS 16
YOU'RE NOT ALONE 18
STAY SAFE! 20
WORDS TO KNOW 22
FOR MORE INFORMATION. 23
INDEX 24

BOLDFACE WORDS APPEAR IN WORDS TO KNOW.

What's a Safety Circle?

A safety circle is group of three to five adults you can trust. Their job is to help keep you safe and happy. The people in your safety circle will always listen to you and believe you. You can tell them anything.

Who's In It?

Can you think of five grown-ups who make you feel safe? Write down their names on a piece of paper. Make sure at least one of the people on your list is not a family member. You could include a teacher, **coach**, or neighbor.

SARAH STAYS SAFE

Sarah has a safety circle. When Sarah is upset about something at home, she talks to her neighbor. When she's worried about school, she talks to her mom. If one member of her safety circle doesn't listen, Sarah can talk to another.

IF ONE MEMBER OF YOUR SAFETY CIRCLE ISN'T HELPING YOU, GO TO THE OTHERS.

THE THREE U'S

When should you use your safety circle? You can use it whenever you like! But it's **especially** important to go to your safety circle when you're feeling one of the three U's: unsafe, **uncomfortable**, or unsure.

WILLA'S WARNING SIGNS

Willa's stomach was turning. Her knees felt weak. Her heart was pounding. Willa felt cold. It was hard to breathe. She wanted to cry. Willa's body was giving her warning signs. Warning signs are your body's way of telling you you're unsafe.

WHAT DO YOUR WARNING SIGNS FEEL LIKE?

FEELINGS ARE FRIENDS

Feelings are your body's way of talking to you. When you feel warning signs, your body is trying to tell you that you're unsafe! Pay attention to when you feel warning signs. Don't **ignore** them. What are you doing? What people are you with?

SHARE YOUR FEELINGS

Cameron was worrying. His friends were all playing a game, but it made him uncomfortable. Cameron didn't know how to tell his friends he didn't like it. Cameron went to his dad. Dad listened. He gave Cameron some ideas of what to do.

IT CAN BE HARD TO STAND UP TO FRIENDS. YOUR SAFETY CIRCLE CAN HELP!

YOU'RE NOT ALONE

Sometimes your safety circle can help you fix a problem. Sometimes, they can just listen! Talking about your feelings out loud can make you feel better. No matter what's going on, don't be afraid. You'll never get in trouble for telling the truth.

DON'T BE AFRAID! YOU'RE NOT ALONE.

STAY SAFE!

Go to your safety circle if you ever feel unsafe, unsure, or uncomfortable. Don't keep secrets from them, even if you're afraid. If one person in your safety circle doesn't listen or doesn't help you, talk to another. Your safety circle is here to help!

Words to Know

coach: The leader of a sports team.

especially: Mainly or most importantly.

ignore: To pretend something isn't happening.

uncomfortable: Feeling unhappy or unsure.

FOR MORE INFORMATION

BOOKS

McAneney, Caitie. *I Talk to Cope*. New York, NY: PowerKids Press, 2023.

Ridley, Sarah. *Being Safe*. New York, NY: PowerKids Press, 2023.

WEBSITES

Kids Health: Talk About Your Feelings
kidshealth.org/en/kids/talk-feelings.html
Learn how to talk about your feelings.

PBS Kids
pbskids.org/video/pbs-kids-talk-about/3043600136
Watch this helpful video of real families talking about their feelings.

Publisher's note to educators and parents: Our editors have carefully reviewed these websites to ensure that they are suitable for students. Many websites change frequently, however, and we cannot guarantee that a site's future contents will continue to meet our high standards of quality and educational value. Be advised that students should be closely supervised whenever they access the internet.

Index

believing, 4
coach, 6
family, 6, 8, 16
feeling afraid, 18, 19, 20
feeling safe, 4, 5, 6
feeling uncomfortable, 10, 11, 16, 20
feeling unsafe, 10, 11, 12, 14, 20
feeling unsure, 10, 11, 20

friends, 16, 17
listening, 4, 18
neighbor, 6, 8
safety circle, 4, 5, 8, 9, 15, 17, 18, 20
secrets, 20
teacher, 6
telling the truth, 18
three U's, 10
warning signs, 12, 13, 14